AF407137

A lone survivor of Viking conquest finds refuge under the care of the knight, Sir Daniel.

For eight long years, Saint Gideon is raised to combat the Viking threat to Wessex and Mercia.

With the help of his mentor, Leviticus, and aid from his new brother, Dan, will these warriors avenge their fellow countrymen?

Or will this endeavor lead to an early grave?

This book is a prequel and takes place eight years before *Blade, Buckler, Bastion/Blade, Buckler, Bastion: The Illuminated Edition.*

It is not essential to read this book first since the events contained are referenced in part, and without spoilers in the next book.

Regardless, this is the first in the book series entitled *Blade, Buckler, Bastion.*

BEFORE, BLADE, BUCKLER, BASTION

Joshua Joseph Montejano

The following is a work of fiction inspired by the historical period known as the Viking Age.

Life was hard. People fought to survive the untamed, natural world.

Cultures clashed. Lives were lost. Cruelties were justified in the brutality of war.

The faith and reason of the people were tested beyond what they could have possibly imagined.

This was the time where everything was filled with uncertainty.

TABLE OF CONTENTS

1. JONAH I...7
2. BROTHERS II..10
3. ISRAEL III..14
4. JOB IV..18
5. GOOD HELGA V..23
6. EPHESIANS VI...28
7. FREYA VII..32
8. FREY VIII..35
9. AXEL-SVEN IX...38
10. PHILIPPIANS X..41
11. SIR DANIEL XI..45
12. FELLOWSHP XII...50
13. ROBERTS XIII...54
14. LEVITICUS I XIV..57
15. JARL LARS XV...62
16. POWERS XVI..66
17. LAMB XVII...70
18. TWINS XVIII...76
19. ANANYA XIX..80
20. OAKEN XX..85
21. PSALMS XXI..88
22. LEVITICUS II XXII......................................93

I

JONAH

The wind howled with a monstrous sigh. The galley ship was almost sinking before the sheer power of the waves. At least sixty enslaved men fought their hardest against the storm. The Viking crew held fast to the ship to brace for impact. They encouraged their cargo to brave the storm.

<u>Jarl Vidar:</u>
Put your backs in it! You too, runt!

The young man rested only for a moment, but that was enough to get a stern look from the jarl. He grabbed the oar once again, with trembling hands. *How long will this misery last*, he thought to himself. His thoughts were quickly blotted out by the sound of a Viking hymn.

IF I WAS TO DIE HERE,
HERE MY BODY LIE,
LOST TO NIFLHEIMR!

MY SOUL LOST AT SEA,
NO LONGER WITH MY KINSMAN,
MY HEART CAN BARELY BARE,

I PRAY YEE-SHALL FIND ME,
BESIDE THE GREAT HALL,

ALAS MY WORDS ARE FLEETING,
I CANNOT HOPE TO LIVE,

HERE MY BODY LIE,
LOST TO NIFLHEIMR!

A cold shiver went down the necks of the of exhausted workers. They did not speak the same language, but the song sounded like the anthem of the dead. The crew stopped rowing altogether.

<u>Jarl Vidar:</u>
What are you doing? Get back to wo-

The ship almost appeared to float in thin air. The ocean had scooped it up higher than the horizon. This lasted but a moment. In that moment, the young man brought his hands together and prayed. All aboard were silent, and the words resonated with them, as if he were speaking to their spirits.

I DON'T KNOW IF YOU'RE REAL OR.....WHO YOU ARE, BUT PLEASE SAVE MY LIFE! I DON'T KNOW WHAT LIES BEYOND THIS LIFE, BUT I FEAR IT IS SOME KIND OF JUDGEMENT!

The ship was taken by the sea.

II

BROTHERS

Saint Gideon awoke from his recurring nightmare. The dream was the oldest memory of his past three long years ago. He was grateful to be in the care of the great Sir Daniel, but he often wondered if there was something more. To his surprise, Leviticus intruded on Saint Gideon's rest to reprimand him.

<u>Leviticus:</u>
For being called the *one-who-cuts-down*…I'm very disappointed in your lack of promptness, Gideon…

<u>St. Gideon:</u>
That's *Saint* to you, Levi!

<u>Leviticus:</u>
And that's Leviticus to you *Saint!*

The two men smiled. They often jested with each other. Regardless, Saint Gideon was late for his morning patrol of the estate. As a mercenary, Leviticus was charged with the security of the estate. He took his job very seriously. While making their way downstairs, Roberts made sure to give ample room for Saint Gideon to pass by him. Saint Gideon took note of it and was very appreciative of this. Unbeknownst to Saint Gideon however, Roberts was very much afraid of him. Roberts was a much older gentlemen servant that feared what he didn't understand, such as Vikings or in Saint Gideon's case, his Haitian origins. He had heard stories of mysticism surrounding the culture and he found the man's skin color off-putting. Roberts would never vocalize his feeling to Sir Daniel. He knew the knight loved Gideon like a second son. As a reward for being a natural with a blade, Sir Daniel even named the intruder Gideon. Although he had mistakenly called Gideon a Saint once, which was more than enough to give Gideon the idea that his name was in fact, Saint Gideon. To name, honor, and give a title to an outsider was unacceptable to Roberts.

Roberts:
If anyone should be a servant, it should be you sir!

Roberts covered his mouth quickly with a cloth. Saint Gideon turned towards Roberts.

St. Gideon:
Yes, we are all servants in a way, Roberts.

Leviticus gave a look of disproval towards Roberts. Saint Gideon was none the wiser.

Roberts:
Well then - If you'll excuse me.

Roberts retreated to the library to fight another day. As Leviticus and Saint Gideon arrived downstairs, they met Helga in the hallway. Saint Gideon continued outside the

mansion to allow Leviticus and the maid have some
privacy.

Helga:
You're too soft on the lad! He's bout…twenty? He needs
more structure!

Leviticus:
I put the iron on him, a bit! He's still Sir Daniel's
favorite…well second favorite. His son Dan is the favorite.

Helga:
He's seventeen? Eighteen? Regardless Dan is younger...
probably. He should be given more grace.

Leviticus:
If it were that simple. He has the weight of his father's
inheritance to consider.

The two grew quieter. They wanted to convey more, but the
words didn't seem to come. Helga shook her head and
changed the subject.

Helga:
I have the reports. It's about the Viking attacks.

Leviticus pushed Helga against the wall and checked to see
if anyone overheard them.

Leviticus:
Go straight to Sir Daniel with this.

<u>Helga:</u>
Alright…I trust you with the information though.

<u>Leviticus:</u>
I know. Just please be discrete, good Helga.

Leviticus covered his mouth to hide his embarrassment for misspeaking. Helga became a bit bashful and decided to tease him.

<u>Helga:</u>
Right away, *good* sir!

Helga waited for Sir Daniel to make his rounds, while Leviticus went to catchup with Saint Gideon. Leviticus came upon Dan and Saint Gideon; they were about to initiate a duel. They stood ready to fight one another in the clearing in front of the manor. Dan attempted to waver Saint Gideon's resolve.

<u>Dan:</u>
You won't humiliate me like you did three years ago!

<u>St. Gideon:</u>
Only if I let you win, brother!

III

ISRAEL

A month after Saint Gideon had washed ashore,
Dan had returned to see the new stranger that sat across the
dinner table conversing with his father.

<u>Dan:</u>
Who is this man? Why is his skin so dark?

<u>St. Gideon:</u>
Why is your skin so pale?

Saint Gideon did not mean to insult Dan, but it came across
that way to the young squire.

<u>Dan:</u>
And so it was *The Lord put a mark on Cain -*

<u>Sir Daniel:</u>
SILENCE! He is not *Cain!* He is foreigner in a strange
land! He is Gideon!

Saint Gideon looked at Sir Daniel with an inquisitive stare.

Sir Daniel:
I'm sorry, Saint Gideon.

Dan:
If he truly lives up to his name, then I challenge this
outsider to a duel!

The sight of a squire in gambeson armor with a buckler and cruciform sword in hand was semi intimidating to Saint Gideon. Although Dan was only about fourteen at the time, so Saint Gideon quickly dismissed this promptly. Besides, the saint was willing and eager to fight another opponent aside from Sir Daniel.

St. Gideon:
Sounds like fun.

The two walked outside with matching weapons to fight in the clearing just before the manor. Sir Daniel thought about de-escalating the situation, but he did want to see how his son would fair against an older and stronger opponent.

Dan:
Your move, *saint!*

Saint Gideon advanced quickly and undaunted. Dan was surprised with his eagerness and instinctively struck with the intention of striking Saint Gideon's right shoulder. Saint Gideon noticed Dan trying to perform guard two, one of the blade and buckler techniques Sir Daniel had taught him shortly after their first meeting. Using his buckler, Saint Gideon successfully deflected the blow and, consequently, threw the squire off balance. At the same

15

time, Saint Gideon placed his left leg behind Dan's right heel, swept him of his feet, while pushing on his opponent's chest, and then recited a victory cry.

St. Gideon:
ISRAEL!

Sir Daniel was impressed by the skill of Saint Gideon, but not by his victory. He felt like chuckling since Israel was not only the blessed land of the Israelites, but it also could refer to being grabbed by the heel. Saint Gideon had essentially said his strategy aloud. How silly, Sir Daniel thought.

Dan:
You're incredible! I've never been beaten so fast. How long will you be staying?

St. Gideon:
I…I don't know…

Saint Gideon began to get nervous. He knew his presence was a bit of a mystery. He worried that he had overstayed his welcome. Sir Daniel noticed his uneasiness and tried to reassure the young man.

Sir Daniel:
As long as he likes. Think of him as an older brother of sorts.

Dan had a look of confusion on his face. He was an only child after all. He quickly gave a grin and began to warm up to the idea.

<u>Dan:</u>
Really? I guess we could always use some extra hands around here. It gets boring just fighting father. Leviticus is away visiting family anyways.

The two young warriors set their weapons aside and shook hands. This was the start of a new relationship. Two strangers had now become brothers.

IV

JOB

Dan rose quickly to his feet. He felt defeated and a bit dizzy to boot. He had lost in the same manner three years prior.

Dan:
Did you just use the same strategy as before?!?

St. Gideon:
You're the one who fell for it.

The moment of reprieve quickly ended with the sight of several dozen Vikings coming over the horizon. The few guards made ready their spears as they pushed Dan and Saint Gideon back into the mansion.

Dan:
I can fight too.

Leviticus:
You can, but there are too many. Hide. We're expecting reinforcements to arrive soon.

Dan:

From whom?

Leviticus made sure the two had made their way inside. To his surprise he too was separated from his men.

Leviticus:

What are you doing? I'm you superior!

The doors were swiftly barricaded from the outside. Saint Gideon and Dan speedily barred the door from the inside as well.

Dan:

I feel like a coward.

St. Gideon:

You're the future. Think of your legacy!

Leviticus:

He's right. We don't have the luxury to dwell on regrets.

A large Viking stepped forth to declare his intentions. The bald jarl stroked his long brown curly beard and spoke with one with authority.

Jarl Lars:

Stand aside! I've come for the head of Sir Daniel!

Brave Guard:

We would never tell you where he was! Even if he was here!

Axel-Sven:
For your sake I suggest you listen to our jarl!

Honorable Guard:
We steel ourselves!

With that the Vikings began their march, slowly backing the fourteen spearmen up against the manor. Leviticus grabbed a great sword above the fireplace, his weapon of choice.

Leviticus:
If they breach the door, then you and I must engage the enemy.

Saint Gideon cleared his throat and saluted Leviticus.

Dan:
Are you too excluding me?

Leviticus looked Dan in the eyes with a look that could kill. Dan retreated to the top of the staircase on the left side. Screams were heard from outside. Leviticus and Saint Gideon retreated to either side of the doors to lie in wait. After quite some time, the door gave way. Leviticus lunged and stabbed through the necks of three large Vikings. They struggled for but a moment and immediately dropped to the ground. With the attention on Leviticus, Saint Gideon followed suit stabbing through the necks of two smaller Vikings. The third was just out of reach. The Viking raised his axe to strike Saint Gideon only to have his head split open by Leviticus. Looking at the carnage caused by the two men, the first row of Vikings stepped back in fear. Two brave Vikings ran in from the second row of warriors. Leviticus blocked the center of the door and raised his sword high above his head. The two berserkers ran with their axes and tried to strike at either of Leviticus's arms. Leviticus took a retreating step and wound his blade in a circular motion back and forth. With his two strikes, the Vikings laid dead before him. Their heads rolled toward their cowardly allies.

<u>Leviticus:</u>
Hell will be full after I'm done with you lot!

Saint Gideon knew Leviticus was a great warrior, but this was still an incredible sight for him to behold. He's like the Israelite war hero, Joshua, he thought to himself.

<u>St. Gideon:</u>
Is not one of you ready to meet their end by our blades?

Two smaller Vikings waded through the crowd to meet the challenge. They were both blonde with similar facial features. Their weapons hidden behind them.

<u>Jarl Lars:</u>
No you too! Stop I forbid you! Frey! Freya!

<u>Freya:</u>
Come now! Let us have a little fun old man.

<u>Axel-Sven:</u>
I'll take the great warrior! Frey you can have the dark one.

<u>Freya:</u>
Come now….what does that leave me?

<u>Axel-Sven:</u>
You can have the boy at the top of the stairs.

Dan was surprised to be noticed. His curiosity had gotten the better of him. His head had poked out from the left hall at the top of the stairs for all to see.

<u>Freya:</u>
Fine. I guess I got first pick before.

Freya made her way through the manor. Protected on either side by Axel-Sven and Frey, she met Dan at the top of the stairs.

<u>Dan:</u>
Stay back, shield-maiden.

Dan was intimidated. She was a bit taller, stronger looking, and wore a blue tunic with blue bindings around her waist. Her legs were protected with a wrap that ended with her boots. Her doppelganger wore similar clothing, but with a red tunic and bindings of the same hue. Freya raised her shield and her long dagger ready to fight her foe. All three duels began. Leviticus, Dan, and Saint Gideon were on their own.

V

GOOD HELGA

Helga entered Sir Daniel's study, ready to give her monthly report to her employer.

Sir Daniel:
Yes? You have the report I imagine.

Helga:
As promised my people appear to be honoring the peace deal you made with them. They plan to visit soon to bring something in good faith.

Sir Daniel:
I'll have to prepare something for the coming days then. I suppose some salted meats would be the safest option. There's no telling when they'll
arrive. Correct?

Helga:
Not long now sir. If they left recently then they might arrive in a day or two.

A huge mass of marching feet could be heard from outside.

Sir Daniel:

That was fast!?!

Shortly after the marching, screams were heard by all the mansion's residents. Sir Daniel drew his cruciform sword and grabbed his heater shield off the counter.

Sir Daniel:

That didn't sound like *good faith!*

Helga:

STAY HERE! I'll check this out for myself!

Sir Daniel:

DO NOT ORDER ME AROUND LIKE A DOG! THIS IS
MY CASTLE!

Helga:

Yes, and the king must always live to see another day. Wait here. I'll go check the back entrance as your contingency warrants. Leviticus and Saint Gideon are no doubt keeping your son safe.

Helga began to undress. Sir Daniel quickly turned away and waited a moment.

Sir Daniel:

Are you decent?

When no answer was given, Sir Daniel turned around out of concern. Helga had changed rather fast using the chest near the corner of the study. She wore mostly brown furs

and some sandals. Her hair was lifted out of the way with
some brown cord.

Sir Daniel:
Quite the disguise! You may need a helmet though.

Helga:
No. I want to be recognized by our people. Besides your
helmet is too big.

After concealing two roundel daggers the spy quickly left
to check the back entrance of the manor past the door of the
study down the stairs through the hall toward a door four
Vikings appeared to be guarding.

Helga:
You four! There's a big chest of gold up here! We'll split it
if you can help me lift it.

Docile Viking:
But Lars wanted us to block this way.

Opportunistic Viking:
More gold for us then!

After the brief debate, all four Vikings began to make their
way upstairs, while walking past Helga. The clever woman
quickly dispatched two of the marauders slitting both of
their necks. The docile Viking slowly turned around in
horror as a dagger met his eye and gut.

Opportunistic Viking:
You mad harpy!

He tried his best to unsheathe the ulfberht sword from its scabbard in time only to be immediately halted after being impaled in both his sword arm and chest. After being thoroughly bathed in the blood of her enemies, Helga decided to drop the first layer of her furs off.

<u>Thyra:</u>
Savages, aren't they?

The old woman had snuck up on Helga unnoticed. She was covered in a large robe with raven feathers attached to the brim of her hood. Her cane had the motif of a raven on the handle. Her frail body and silver hair spoke of her experience. Should I kill her, Helga pondered.

<u>Thyra:</u>
There were four of them. Disgusting. To think they would try to take you before your wedding day.

Helga let her guard down. The situation had been completely misinterpreted. This was to Helga's advantage. She decided to play along. Crocodile tears began to stream down Helga's face.

<u>Helga:</u>
I was so scared! How could this happen to me?!?

<u>Thyra:</u>
Now, now deary it'll be alright. Come join me and the shield-maidens outside. I wish to comfort you.

Helga knew this was her chance to slip amongst the ranks of her enemies. She made her way past the old woman.

26

Helga blacked out after receiving a sharp blow to the head.

VI

EPHESIANS

To Helga, she appeared to be floating in thin air. She bore witness to a familiar scene from her past. It was the first time she had met Leviticus. She silently watched the event unfold. Leviticus stood tall and at attention guarding the front door to the manor. He saw the young Helga walk by.

<u>Leviticus:</u>
Where are you going, miss.

<u>Helga:</u>
I have news for Sir Daniel.

<u>Leviticus:</u>
A Dane? The peace is finally here, I'd surmise.

<u>Helga:</u>
I'm Norwegian.

Leviticus tried to come up it an insulting remark to his former enemy until he had made eye contact with her. Her eyes were a dark brown, her hair of the same hue, curly and untamed. She looked strong and confident. Leviticus had never seen such a woman before.

Leviticus:
So beautiful.

Helga began to twirl the ends of her locks between her fingers. She smiled at the young warrior.

Helga:
You jest?

Leviticus leaned forward while resting on his great sword. He gave the woman his full and undivided attention.

Leviticus:
I do not, *jest.*

Helga blushed. She had many men call her beautiful, but never one she found to be to her liking. He was certainly the youngest man to show interest in her.

Leviticus:
Any man in your life?

Helga:
Lots of offers. From men twice my age or more.

Leviticus:
But your…. twenty or so?

29

Helga:
And that's the shame of it all. Too old for a young man.
Too old for someone my own age.

Leviticus:
I'm about thirty, but I wouldn't mind you.

Roberts had been standing near the doorway for quite some time. He decided to voice his concerns to the lovebirds.

Roberts:
Don't associate with the help, Leviticus.

Leviticus:
Roberts, you're the help.

Roberts:
Fine. Don't associate with the Dane.

Leviticus & Helga:
Norwegian!

Roberts rolled his eyes and made his way back inside the manor. He was done with what he considered a pointless argument.

Helga:
I must see Sir Daniel now.

Leviticus:
Of course, go right ahead, spy.

<u>Helga:</u>
How did you?

<u>Leviticus:</u>
What else could you be?

Helga put her finger near her mouth signaling for Leviticus to keep quiet about the matter. Leviticus gave her a quick wink. What a pleasant dream, thought the observing Helga.

VII

FREYA

Dan deflected Freya's stabbing motion with his sword and buckler. He had fought many opponents before, but never in a life and death battle.

<u>Freya:</u>
You're pretty good! Pretty handsome too…That's too bad.

Dan was reluctant to respond to the shield-maiden. He was focused on trying to stay alive. Her attack patterns were predictable, but she had a strength to her that could easily overpower the squire if he was not careful enough. Dan winced in pain on account of his ankle. Saint Gideon had given Dan quite the thrashing earlier. Freya noticed this and kicked him in the side of his injured leg. She meant to throw him off balance for a more lethal strike. She was surprised when Dan fell to the ground. Freya had already moved in to run the lad through. She quickly changed her strategy when she saw Dan's blade extending toward her as he was falling. Freya quickly retracted her blade and moved her shield closer to herself. The shield-maiden began to fall toward the warrior as well. She had overcommitted to have a killing blow. Dan's sword had slashed the woman just above her pelvis. She rolled off to the side and out of

harm's way. If it were not for her shield catching the blow
and glancing off, she would have had a deeper cut.

Dan:
A female warrior, really? I thought you were just a myth.

Freya looked toward Dan inquisitively. She wondered how
Dan was willing to still make banter after so many close
calls.

Freya:
You're lucky to still be alive, boy!

Dan paused for a moment and gave Freya a look of
confusion, then responded to her promptly.

Dan:
I could say the same to you, miss.

To take the squire by surprise, the she-warrior pretended to
rise and fall and then immediately leapt toward her foe with
dagger in hand. Without thinking, Dan rolls off to the side
while barely avoiding being impaled. Freya's blow causes
her dagger to get caught in the railing. Freya lifts her head
towards Dan and tries her best to pry her weapon from the
railing. Dan instinctively moves into guard one and lunges
to stab Freya. He stops just before reaching her face. After
looking her in the eyes, Dan feels a tightness in his chest.
She's so beautiful, it would be a waste to kill her, Dan
thought to himself.

Dan:
I've never met someone as beautiful as you are before.

<u>Freya:</u>

What does that matter now? You're going to kill me, right?

The squire examined the tip of his sword thoroughly. Dan thought about the deed and then shook his head in discontent. His eyes returned to her with conviction behind his words.

<u>Dan:</u>

No I won't.

Freya's fear had now been replaced with pure rage. She had never felt so insulted and humiliated in in her entire life. She interpretated Dan's mercy as a direct attack.

<u>Freya:</u>

So, you'd shame me then. Denying me a warrior's death? You savage!

<u>Dan:</u>

Your people told you to kill me, right? My quarrel isn't with you. It's with your jarl. You don't have to follow him.

The shield-maiden became even more distraught. Surely, this squire knew that a jarl's will was absolute. This fool is trying to catch me off guard, Freya concluded. Freya tried to retrieve her weapon once more, but to no avail. Assuming her weapon was out of commission, Freya ran toward Dan with both hands free. Her intention was to ring the warrior's neck. Dan was taken off guard and stood paralyzed with fear.

VIII
FREY

Saint Gideon and Frey locked their blades together. Each warrior wanted to gauge their opponent's strength before going in for the killing blow. Neither was willing to give way. The safety of the bind was something warriors understood. Tired of the quiet, Frey was the first to break the silence between the two of them.

<u>Frey:</u>
So…You are as tough as you look.

Saint Gideon was surprised by his foe's strength as well, especially for one of small stature. He was more surprised by his voice.

<u>St. Gideon:</u>
Huh? You're a man?

The saint was legitimately shocked. His face was very similar to the shield-maiden's, so he thought they were sisters. Frey was cross with the warrior. He lashed out with abandon. While keeping one dagger locked with Saint Gideon's sword, Frey took his other weapon and tried to penetrate Saint Gideon through his chest. In response, the saint smacked Frey across the face with his buckler. Frey was astounded when no blood dripped from Saint Gideon's breast.

Frey:

What sorcery is this? Surely, your armor is soft.

Saint Gideon inspected his lamellar armor cuirass that he often had hidden under his gambeson. It was now dented, but still intact. He gave a sigh of relief. He was once gored by a boar before. After that, Saint Gideon wore his armor quite often. Saint Gideon had finished his inspection and decided to respond to Frey's question.

St. Gideon:

Deus meus, Deus meus, in quo speravi, scutum meum et cornu salutis meae!

Frey:

I won't let you caste another spell! Witch!

St. Gideon:

My God is my rock, in whom I take refuge, my shield and the horn of my salvation!

Frey:

Now you preach to me! You are two-faced! Do you mock me?!?

Frey rushed the saint, extending both daggers towards his face. Saint Gideon tried to defend with his buckler. He had his sword ready and hidden behind his buckler in guard six. Saint Gideon blocked one strike only to be surprised with

36

the other dagger moving towards his unarmored left thigh. *This blow may well cripple me,* Saint Gideon predicted.

IX

AXEL-SVEN

Leviticus's great sword and Axel-Sven's axe and knife were locked in, with little give. The mercenary was surprised that the smaller Viking was able to hold his own against a stronger opponent.

Leviticus:
Your technique is something else, Dane.

Leviticus was very surprised with the Viking's resistance. Most of Leviticus's opponents tended to die quickly. This was a chance for the mercenary to truly test his metal.

Axel-Sven:
I've killed men like you with ease. You've lasted longer than I…Dane? We're Swedes not Danes.

Leviticus was puzzled. He didn't seem to know the difference. To him the only different people he had met before were the Danes, Helga, and Saint Gideon.

Leviticus:
What's the difference?

Axel-Sven's face had turned bright red. He intended to repay the insult in kind. Axel-Sven ran his axe across Leviticus's blade, while bringing his knife straight towards his opponent's face. Leviticus tried to retract his sword to gain a reach advantage, but this was countered by Axel-Sven's quick thinking. Leviticus's sword was now hooked by the axe and held in place by the knife. Stepping on the mercenary's foot, Axel-Sven bashed his head into his foe's skull. The Swede struggled to keep on his feet. If he hadn't known better, he'd surmise that he had hit a brick wall. The swede fell to the ground, barely clutching his weapons.

<u>Axel-Sven:</u>
How can he be like steel?

Leviticus performed a knocking action on the left side of his navy-blue starfish hat. A muffled echo of armor reverberating could be heard.

<u>Leviticus:</u>
It's called a secret helm, but don't tell anyone.

Axel-Sven rose quickly to meet Leviticus in combat once more. Leviticus, with his blade fully extended, met the challenge. Axel-Sven successfully deflected the sword off to the side meeting the mercenary head-on. Still dazed by the attack, Axel-Sven misses Leviticus's face. Both his weapons bounce of the mercenaries' helm. Without thinking, Leviticus headbutts Axel-Sven's skull. The Viking suddenly drops. His head broke his fall. Sanguine liquid stains the Viking's face. As a worthy opponent, Leviticus felt the need to say something. He then stopped himself, realizing the gap between them.

<u>Leviticus:</u>
Prayers are for the living. Not the dead. Hell has you now,
Swede.

X
PHILIPPIANS

To the saint's surprise, the fight had stopped. Frey looked in his sister's direction in horror and watched the scene unfold. Frey could barely speak. Freya spat out crimson liquid covering Dan in a thick layer of her blood. Freya had accidentally run herself through on Dan's blade.

<u>Freya:</u>
I'm afraid to die….

<u>Dan:</u>
I'll pray for you. I'm here.

Never in her life had Freya experienced such compassion. She was compelled to act. Freya put her arms around Dan's neck. Dan seemed surprised. He was afraid until her lips met his for a moment. She fell to the ground. Dan bent down to meet her and said a prayer as she lay dying.

<u>Dan:</u>
Sic enim Deus dilexit mundum, ut filium suum unigenitum daret, ut omnis qui credit in eum non pereat, sed habeat vitam aeternam.

Freya was mesmerized by his words, but she gave Dan a look of perplexity in response to her lack of understanding Latin.

<u>Dan:</u>
For God so loved the world that he gave his one and only Son, that whoever believes in him shall not perish but have eternal life.

<u>Freya:</u>
I accept.

Dan was shocked, he didn't think that a Viking would believe in his God after a lifetime of probably only knowing gods like Thor and Odin. Shocked, but relieved. Dan was truly worried for this woman's soul.

<u>Freya:</u>
If he's anything like you, then I'd like to meet him. His name. Was it Jesus? Jesus Christ?

Freya spat out a generous portion of blood and then was silent.

<u>Frey:</u>
Sister? What have you done?

Frey extended what was left of his right arm toward his sister. Until that moment he had not realized that Saint Gideon had severed it whilst he was distracted. Losing the will to fight, Frey loosened the grip in his left hand, and dropped his other weapon. Saint Gideon caught the Viking as he fell.

42

<u>Frey:</u>

Where you have gone, I cannot follow.

<u>St. Gideon:</u>

If you call out to the same God, you will see her again.

Saint Gideon knew God was forgiving, but he did not know to what extent. What he did know was that Hell was a place one would not wish for their worst enemy. He hoped for the best.

<u>Frey:</u>

Then maybe I will…

The color faded from Frey's eyes. His body lay motionless on the floor. The Vikings were silent for but a moment and then sung a funeral song.

Valhalla be,
Me destiny,

Halls of gold,
For young and old,

We wait by the fire,
Till we expire,

A sword in hand,
He does demand,

For halls of gold,
For young and old,
Valhalla,

Two dozen unarmed Vikings entered the mansion unopposed; they retreated outside to prepare the proper funeral rites. Jarl Lars was at a loss for words. He had come all this way and lost three of his best warriors and for what? The pain in his right knee caused him to nearly fall to the ground. He reassured himself, Sir Daniel must pay.

SIR DANIEL

It was a cold a bloodied night on the day of Jarl Lars's fateful encounter with Sir Daniel. Both warriors were in their prime. The Viking had his ulfberht sword and shield extended toward the knight. Sir Daniel met his foe with his heater shield and cruciform sword.

Sir Daniel:
Your army is decimated. You have been left behind. Surrender.

To show his dissatisfaction, the jarl spat a large and disgusting mass of blood and mucus at the knights' feet.

Jarl Lars:
Surrender? To you? I'd rather die!

Roberts:
I'd like to slay him if he won't surrender.

Sir Daniel:
No Roberts, you can barely stand.

In Roberts's pursuit of vengeance, he had neglected to notice his wounds from the long day of battle. He held his left arm in agony and tried to rebandage it. He tried to stand once more, but his right ancle appeared to have been twisted as well. Sir Daniel watched what was left of the jarl's men flee in the distance. Leviticus and his men began to march towards the jarl all at once. Sir Daniel waved them off. Leviticus reluctantly told his men to stand down. The mercenary was not one for duels when victory was assured by overwhelming force.

<u>Sir Daniel:</u>
Fine. If you won't listen to reason, then fight me.

<u>Jarl Lars:</u>
Glady!

Sir Daniel hid his sword behind his shield and held the blade in reverse. Jarl Lars didn't know how to respond to such a perverse method of sword combat. The Viking hid his doubts and concerns, stepping forward while presenting both shield and sword in front of him. Stepping to the side, Sir Daniel avoided the attack while extending his own blade and allowing it to pass by the heater shield. The jarl tried to defend his head. He soon regretted it when he realized the knight was leading him. The knight's blade contacted his foe's mail, sliding off instead of piercing, and was redirected into the Viking's right knee. Jarl Lars dropped his weapons, unable to continue the attack.

<u>Jarl Lars:</u>
My leg! What have you done?!?

Sir Daniel:
I'll ask you again. Surrender?

Jarl Lars:
Kill me! Don't dishonor me! Kill me!

Roberts went to grant the jarl's request, only to be halted by Leviticus.

Roberts:
Out of my way, Mercian.

Roberts pushed on Leviticus with great effort. He grabbed his injured shoulder remembering his wounds.

Leviticus:
Wessex is my home. The same as you.

Leviticus Gripped Roberts's wound tightly. He forced the servant to remember his condition.

Roberts:
I'll cut you down if you get in my –

Leviticus tripped the servant with little effort, catching him before he received further injury.

Leviticus:
You're half a corpse. Sit down and shut up. Your knight
has made his decision.

Roberts had begun to lose consciousness. His spirit was willing, but his flesh had failed him. The battle was over

47

for the servant. Sir Daniel was distracted by the two warriors for a moment, he regained focus on the jarl. The Viking tried to regrip his sword, but it was a fool's errand. Jarl Lars talked under his breath.

<u>Jarl Lars:</u>
How can I go to the great hall without my sword in hand.

<u>Sir Daniel:</u>
Are you…giving up?

<u>Jarl Lars:</u>
No! Bind my sword to my hand and slay me!

Sir Daniel scratched his head in with indecision. He found Viking warriors to be very strange. He was always overwhelmed by their bizarre rituals.

<u>Sir Daniel:</u>
You can't fight. You won't stop fighting though. I guess I must take you to the king.

Without thinking words began to come from the jarl's mouth as if an outside power had caused him to speak in a threatening and outlandish way.

IF YOU DENY ME MY HOME,

IN THE GROUND YOU WILL LAY,

DENY ME MY HOME, IT IS YOU I WILL SLAY,

I SWEAR ON THIS DAY, I WILL NOT STOP TILL YOU FALL BY MY BLADE!

Jarl Lars was exhausted from the great battle; his head was spinning, he was injured, and had barely regained control of himself. Sir Daniel didn't know how to respond to jarl's sudden attempt to curse or threaten him. This was Sir Daniel's most confusing interaction with a Viking. The knight shrugged and took his sword pommel striking the jarl with a sharp blow to the head. Incapacitated, the jarl could do nothing. The warriors carried the jarl, Roberts, and their wounded off the battlefield. Sir Daniel would have honored the Viking's wish if he had known what was to come.

XII
FELLOWSHIP

The lord of the manor paced back and forth, unable to keep his mind at ease. He could not help but hear many of the events that had transpired that day. Grabbing his chest, Sir Daniel suppressed the urge to strike down his enemies.

<u>Sir Daniel:</u>
If I fight, surely, I will die. Their numbers are too great.

Sir Daniel felt like a coward. He often fought on the battlefield, but this was different. This was an execution.

<u>Dan:</u>
Father! You're safe. Thank God!

Sir Daniel was surprised to see his son and two of his best warriors enter his study undetected.

<u>Roberts:</u>
Thank Roberts.

Two Vikings lay dead near the servant's feet. Roberts
casually continued to clean the blood off his mace. He tried
not to make eye contact with Saint Gideon.

St. Gideon:
They seem to be having a funeral outside. It's getting dark
too. Maybe they'll attack again tomorrow.

Sir Daniel:
What we need is time. Let's pray you're right then.

Roberts:
Reinforcements should be here by then…. hopefully.

Leviticus:
Wait! Where's Helga?

Sir Daniel:
I thought she regrouped with you.

Roberts:
She probably brought them here in the first place. She's
Dane after all.

Leviticus:
She's Norwegian. She's still one of us. If it wasn't for her,
we wouldn't have reinforcements.

Roberts:
Let's hope our deal with the devil saves us.

Leviticus:
Bite your tongue. She's, my wife!

Roberts gave a surprised look towards Leviticus. He did not know how to respond to such a revelation. Pushing Leviticus while leaving the room, Roberts set off to take the first watch. Leviticus thought of defending his wife's honor, but he knew now was not the time to fight amongst one another.

<u>St. Gideon:</u>
We all knew you were fond of her, but marriage?

<u>Dan:</u>
Hey! You said I could marry her.

<u>Leviticus:</u>
I was joking. You were thirteen and she was twenty at the time. Did you really think…If it makes you feel any better, we signed the papers; we just haven't had a ceremony yet.

<u>St. Gideon & Sir Daniel:</u>
You have my blessing.

<u>Dan:</u>
Fine, whatever. You have my blessing.

<u>Sir Daniel:</u>
When we get through this, I'll throw a big wedding for you.
Mark my words.

<u>Leviticus:</u>
In all honesty…I hope she did leave the manor and abandon us. She means the world to me.

Sir Daniel:

Knowing her, she probably already slipped out and met up
with her people.

St. Gideon:

Sure, she's probably on her way now.

Leviticus:

If that's the case, we should wait for the time being.

Roberts had listened to the last of the conversation while
waiting outside the doorway of the study. He waited for the
conversation to end and then made his way to the stairs
leading to the entrance. He wondered why Sir Daniel would
forgive the sins of the Norwegian Vikings. Their
relationship was beneficial, but Roberts couldn't look
beyond their past transgressions. Saint Gideon walked out
of the study for a moment to gather his thoughts, only to be
surprised by Roberts words.

Roberts:

They destroyed my home. They killed my friends, my wife,
and I must make friends with them? Why don't I just drink
poison while I'm at it.

Roberts:

Jarl Vidar is a stain on this earth.

Saint Gideon whispered to himself. His thoughts
overwhelmed him.

St. Gideon:

Jarl Vidar, that name seems so familiar…Why is that?

XIII

ROBERTS

The two newlyweds hid in the cramped confines of the wardrobe, hoping and praying to be safe from the Viking's heard next door pillaging their neighbors.

Lilith:
What do we do? Margret is in danger.

Roberts:
There are too many my love. She's done for. We will be too if we interfere.

Roberts held Lilith in his arms, hoping this would not be their final moments. Three Vikings had made their way through the door. Roberts and Lilith could hear the trio looking for valuables just downstairs.

Lilith:
Roberts. I'm scared.

Roberts:
We'll be fine darling. We just must hide for a little while longer.

Jarl Vidar:

I'll check the upstairs. Maybe there's something of worth up there.

The couple held their breath as the jarl made his way up the stairs and into the bedroom. He looked in the drawers, he looked under the bed and he tried to open the wardrobe without any success.

Jarl Vidar:

Piece of junk. No lock either?

Jarl Vidar began to walk out of the room when he heard a sigh of relief coming from the wardrobe. In response, the Viking hurled his axe into the furniture. He walked over to the wardrobe to retrieve his weapon with little luck.

Greedy Viking:

Come next door! There's gold here jarl!

Jarl Vidar left his axe and raced out the home along with his two warriors. Roberts gave a sigh of relief.

Roberts:

You almost gave us away, my love.

Lilith did not answer. Her eyes no longer moved, and her body started to buckle.

Roberts:

Lilith, are you hurt?

Roberts neglected to notice that the axe had penetrated the wardrobe and had plunged partway into his wife's spine.

Roberts:
I'll kill them. I'll kill them all!

It had seemed like an eternity, locked within the confines of the wardrobe. Roberts kept replaying the events in his head, trying to see if there was another way. He barely noticed the loud noise of the doors being pried off at the hinges. The door gave way revealing Sir Daniel to be the culprit. Roberts was stuck in the wardrobe for two days until Sir Daniel had arrived. He had heard word of the Viking attack near his lands.

Sir Daniel:
My word! You're alive!

Speechless Robert continued to hold the body of his beloved. Sir Daniel inferred the connection.

Sir Daniel:
Let's find the man that did this to your wife. Come on.

Roberts grabbed the knight's hand and left with him. Indebted to the knight, Roberts pledged his service to Sir Daniel. Roberts regretted that decision later when the peace talks started. The death of Jarl Vidar at sea helped to lesson the servants rage for a while.

LEVITICUS I

Helga awoke in the dew of the new day. She was surprised to have her hands unbound. The old woman from before watched her with curiosity.

Thyra:
Finally awake, deary?

Helga:
I shouldn't have let my guard down around you.

Thyra:
Yes, that's true. I believe introductions are in order. I'm the seer Thyra.

Helga:
I'm Helga.

The old woman involuntarily spat out her soup in response.

Thyra:
Helga? Helga, HELGA? You work at the manor? The spy?

<u>Helga:</u>
Yes? Isn't that why you attacked me?

<u>Thyra:</u>
I thought you were a Swede. I was going to make you give
me some intel.

<u>Helga:</u>
So you're with the reinforcements?!?

<u>Thyra:</u>
Shush! The others haven't shown up yet. I'm lying low.
You should too if you know what's good for you.

Jarl Lars had arrived on scene and issued his commands to
his forces.

<u>Jarl Lars</u>:
Finish your breakfast! We attack soon!

He saw Thyra in the distance and came to meet her.

<u>Jarl Lars</u>:
Woman! Where is Axel-Sven?

<u>Thyra:</u>
We couldn't find the body after we carried him out. A bear
must have got him.

<u>Jarl Lars:</u>
May the gods forgive us. How are supposed to give him a
funeral without the body?

Thyra:

As I said before, I am a seer. I'll make sure the gods accept him into Valhalla. You have my word.

Jarl Lars uncharacteristically bowed to the seer in appreciation. He walked in front of the manor to voice his demands.

Jarl Lars:

Come out! Or we will burn the mansion to the ground! We know you're in there!

Leviticus walked outside alone and unarmed. Helga tried to run towards her husband until Thyra interfered.

Thyra:
You're of no use to him dead.

Helga began tear up and quickly wiped them away out of fear of being seen by the Vikings.

Helga:
But I must.

Thyra violently pulled Helga back to the log she was sitting on, almost knocking her down in the process.

Thyra:
You can't.

Leviticus surveyed the grounds carefully and continued to approach Jarl Lars while making his offer.

<u>Leviticus:</u>
You may kill me if you wish, but I have a request.

<u>Jarl Lars:</u>
That being?

<u>Leviticus:</u>
Let the rest of my men go free. And my wife as well.
Helga.

Saint Gideon, Sir Daniel, Roberts, and Dan watched as Leviticus stepped out of the manor. They thought to call out to him, and change his mind, but they knew he was a man of great resolve.

<u>Jarl Lars:</u>
Fine I promise to spare your wife.

Four Vikings flanked the mercenary on either side and brought him before the jarl.

<u>Jarl Lars:</u>
Bring the firewood. We will burn him alive. Hurry. Then, find and burn the rest.

<u>Leviticus:</u>
You said you would spare them.

<u>Jarl Lars:</u>
Your wife. Your wife. I said I'd spare your wife.

Leviticus thought to lie if only to delay the tyrants need for revenge.

<u>Leviticus:</u>
SHE'S INSIDE RIGHT NOW!

Jarl Lars noticed the warrior's sudden change of tone.

<u>Jarl Lars:</u>
I know a liar when I see one! You think me to be a fool?!?

Helga tried her best to not attempt a rescue, especially when making a fire would take some time. Reinforcements should be here soon, she reassured herself. Thyra looked her in the eyes and nodded as an attempt to reassure her.

JARL LARS

It was now midday. The preparations had been made. Jarl Lars sat upon a stump with a purple cushion on top, ready to see the show. Leviticus had a less comfortable seat comprised of the tree he was now bound to and the piles of wood flanking him on either side.

Jarl Lars:
You kill my men! You kill Axel-Sven, my right-hand man! You people send both my children to Helheim! So now I burn you alive! Have your people watch! Then, I kill them too!

Leviticus:
You refuse to fight me in duel out of fear! So, you tie me to this tree and execute me! You're no warrior!

Jarl Lars took hold of his right knee. He squeezed it and rubbed it to suppress the pain. His days of fighting had long passed.

Jarl Lars:
I'm jarl! I'm king! Kill him.

A Viking came forth with a torch ready to perform the
execution. Helga ran to the site and pleaded for the trial
judgement to stop.

Helga:

You can't kill him! Don't kill Leviticus! Please, he's, my
husband!

Jarl Lars:

My word is law. I don't go back on my word.

He looked into the woman's eyes. He saw the anguish
behind them. The jarl felt guilt of what he was about to do,
but his anger was still greater than his moral compass.

Jarl Lars:

I'm feeling generous. You may speak Leviticus? Then we
kill you.

Helga tried to get closer to her husband, but the jarl
motioned for her to step back.

Jarl Lars:

Just Leviticus may speak.

Leviticus began to speak. He decided to pray the longest
prayer he could think of to delay his execution. Something
he often heard Saint Gideon pray in times of distress. He
wasn't too sure about his Latin, but he figured that the
longer the better.

Pater noster qui in caelis est.
sanctificetur nomen tuum;

adveniat regnum tuum
fiat voluntas tua;
in terra sicut in caelo.

Panem nostrum quotidianum
Da nobis hodie.
et dimitte nobis debita nostra
sicut et nos dimittimus
debitoribus nostris.

Et ne nos inducas in
tentationem.
sed libera nos malo

Si enim dimisertis homnibus
Peccantibus in vos, dimettet
vobis et Pater vester coelestis.
Si autem non demiseritis aliis,
Pater vester non demittet
peccata vestra

Our Father in heaven,
hallowed be your name,
your kingdom come,
your will be done,
on earth as it is in heaven.

Give us today our daily bread.
And forgive us our debts,
as we also have forgiven our debtors.

And lead us not into temptation,
but deliver us from the evil one.

For if you forgive other people when they sin against you, your heavenly Father will also forgive you. But if you do not forgive others their sins, your Father will not forgive your sins.

Jarl Lars:
Enough! Begin the execution!

Leviticus closed his eyes. He waited for the end to come. He continued to wait for what seemed like an eternity. Did it really take that long to start an oil fire over some wood, he questioned. The mercenary opened his eyes to investigate. Something was different. No, everything is the same, he thought. Time appeared to have stopped right before Leviticus's eyes. He was still conscious, but he could barely move. The air was surprisingly cold as well. His eyes scanned the environment. Nothing seemed to have changed.

Leviticus:
Is this Divine intervention?

Voice:
YOU MAY CALL IT THAT MORTAL.

Frozen in fear, the warrior could barely speak. The air in his lunges had left him. His skull felt as though it was about to burst. He frantically looked for the origin of the voice in question. When he saw the visage, he could barely stand to be in its presence.

POWERS

The shadowy figure looked the mortal in his eyes. Leviticus tried to avert his gaze, but he feared that looking away may somehow spell his doom.

Visage:
I HAVE A PROPOSITION FOR YOU, LEVITICUS.

Leviticus pretended not to hear, even when blood began to flow out from his ears. He waited and hoped that the visage would leave.

Visage:
GIVE ME YOUR FEALTY AND I WILL SAVE YOUR LIFE.

Leviticus:
And…take….my……soul?

Visage:
NO A FAVOR. A FAVOR IS ALL I ASK.

Leviticus:
N- no…

<u>Visage:</u>
THINK OF YOUR FRIENDS. THINK OF YOUR WIFE.
THINK OF YOUR CHILD.

<u>Leviticus:</u>
My child?

<u>Visage:</u>
IF NOT FOR YOU. THEN, FOR THEM.

Leviticus was silent. He closed his eyes to think. He was afraid to die, but he was more afraid of losing himself. Once again, he prayed. Not to delay or make excuses, but because he remembered that was what his good friend Saint Gideon often did when he needed answers.

<u>Visage:</u>
STOP YOUR FOOLISHNESS! NO ONE'S COMING TO
SAVE YOU! YOU CAN BARELY SPEAK! WHO
COULD REACH YOU!?!

<u>Leviticus:</u>
I command -

Leviticus started to choke. His words had eluded him.

<u>Visage:</u>
I CAN STOP HIS HEART, OR I CAN STOP YOURS.
YOUR CHOICE!

Leviticus had remembered the visage from before. He spoke in Jarl Lar's stead at the battle on the day of Sir Daniel's victory. This gave Leviticus the resolve he needed.

67

<u>Leviticus:</u>
I command you to leave and to go back to the one that sent
you.

<u>Visage:</u>
I WILL KILL YOU BEFORE YOU MAKE ME LEAVE!
YOU WILL DIE EITHER WAY.

A new voice had overtaken Leviticus. The visage in turn began to cower in fear and great anguish came upon him.

Call upon my name and you will be saved.

Leviticus began feel his life slip away as he drifted in and out of consciousness. He hastily said the first words that came to him.

*IN THE NAME
THAT IS ABOVE
ALL NAMES,*

*I COMMAND YOU
TO LEAVE AND
NEVER RETURN!*

XVII

LAMB

The torch bearer threw his instrument of destruction behind him in fear after hearing Leviticus's commanding and undaunted words, combined with his bloodied and distraught looking expression. To the Viking, it was as though his foe had made the transformation of a lamb to a lion. Jarl Lars caught the torch on his face. He gave a blood curdling scream as the flame scarred the right side of his face. As he stomped and frantically tried to fan the flames on his face, the jarl had put out the torch by way of kicking up dirt below him. Another Viking grabbed the torch with the intention of relighting it. An arrow to the chest made short work of him.

Sir Daniel:
There's more where that came from!

Sir Daniel, Dan, and Roberts stood their ground, ready to send another arrow down towards their foes from the safety of the manor's balcony.

Jarl Lars:
Sir Daniel, fight me like a man!

The jarl stood up quickly only to fall to his wounded knee. This enraged him more than the burns he had received. His leg was a constant reminder of his defeat to Sir Daniel and an end to his days as a warrior.

Jarl Lars:
You dishonored me as a warrior and expect me to spare you?

Sir Daniel:
I let you live and left you to the king. I *spared* you.

Jarl Lars:
You should have killed me! Now you will pay for killing my men, my righthand man, and my children.

Dan and Saint Gideon made eye contact, knowing full well that the twins were of the same blood as the jarl. How could the jarl let something like that go, they both concluded. Saint Gideon made up his mind and ran down the stairs and began to leave the manor.

Sir Daniel:
I promise you my riches, my armor, anything you need, but my lineage must continue.

The jarl was furious with the knight's remark. He didn't see why his kin should die, but Sir Daniel's son should live. He meant to vocalize his disapproval until he saw Saint Gideon appear before him.

<u>St. Gideon:</u>
I offer myself up to you, jarl. Perhaps another man will allow your rage to be properly satiated.

Given this opportunity, Thyra thought to delay the jarl further. She remembered a story she heard from the Christians.

<u>Thyra:</u>
I've heard stories of this one my jarl. A great warrior with the strength of kings as if Sampson in the flesh, as the Christians would say.

Jarl Lars looked Saint Gideon in the eyes. The young warrior never left Jarl Lars' gaze. The jarl assumed Saint Gideon must be the descendant of this foreign sounding warrior.

<u>Jarl Lars:</u>
This one. I see no fear in him. How would I take pleasure in my revenge?

<u>Thyra:</u>
Suffering perhaps?

Jarl Lars was pleased with this solution. He pried the old woman further.

<u>Jarl Lars:</u>
What then do you propose seer?

<u>Thyra:</u>
Hurt the source of his power. Demoralize him. Have him beg for his own death and then deny him even that.

The woman leaned in close and whispered instructions to the jarl. Jarl Lars decided that her methods were to his liking.

<u>Jarl Lars:</u>
Come here, Sampson!

Saint Gideon assumed the command was for him and stepped forward to meet the jarl. Two Vikings pushed Saint Gideon to the ground. The jarl took a knife and held it over the saint's head.

<u>Jarl Lars:</u>
I will spare this man's life! In return, I take the source of his power!

Saint Gideon knew the biblical story of Sampson quite well. It only occurred to him at that moment what was about to happen. He decided to bear the pain of what was to transpire if only to appease the jarl and to buy time for reinforcements to arrive. His allies stood by knowing full well this was the only way their friend may be spared. Slowly and meticulously, the jarl began to remove bits of hair and flesh from the top of the warrior's head. Saint Gideon gritted his teeth; this alone was not enough to endure the pain of his suffering. He said a silent prayer to keep his mind distracted and to lessen the pain of the experience.

Helga and Leviticus looked in horror as they had the best view of their friend's anguish. Sir Daniel and Dan tried to avert their gaze but could not abandon their own blood. Roberts averted his gaze completely, biting his lip to keep his calm. The jarl gave a smile, admiring his work. He delighted in the tears and blood of the man that stood before him.

<u>Jarl Lars:</u>
Weak as a day-old pup! I'd do you a favor by killing you! I refuse to give you even that kindness!

Jarl Lars took his time to enjoy the torment he had inflicted upon the warrior. The two Vikings had let go of Saint Gideon. He puked and had lost consciousness. The jarl kicked Saint Gideon waking him up in the process. An arrow flew past the jarl's head, taking his right ear. At that moment the jarl signaled to his spearmen. Five spears were thrown toward the culprit. Roberts fell to the floor after receiving two spears in his stomach.

Roberts died quickly with a smile on his face. His allies were surprised by his actions. He had always hated Saint Gideon. Jarl Lars gave an expression of delight. He drifted off for but a moment, wondering if he should have told his three best warriors to stay behind, especially his two kin that had seemed a bit out of place before the raid.

XVIII

TWINS

Frey and Freya sat around the fire. They had made camp in the forest not too far off from Sir Daniel's estate. Freya was nervous, she looked to her brother for his advice.

<u>Freya:</u>
Should we….be doing this?

Frey knew from very little information what his sister meant. As twins, they knew each other quite well.

<u>Frey:</u>
You love testing your skills in battle, but you don't like the reasoning behind it. Is that right?

She looked away. Freya knew a warrior wasn't supposed to have this kind of doubt.

<u>Frey:</u>
I think of it this way.

Frey stood up and tried to sound convincing to Freya and himself.

<u>Frey:</u>
If it weren't for the politics, petty squabbles, and revenge, we would never get the chance to test our skills in real combat.

<u>Axel-Sven:</u>
I never ask why. That's the job of our jarl. My conscious is clean. My actions are limited. Don't over think it, fair shield-maiden.

The twins were surprised to see Axel-Sven listen in on their conversation. Luckily, he had always been a good friend to the two. He may have been their only friend for that matter.

<u>Freya:</u>
You always seem to comfort us when the others avoid us like the plague. Why is that?

<u>Frey:</u>
That's an understatement. If we weren't the jarl's blood, we'd probably be put to death for being cursed or something.

<u>Axel-Sven:</u>
I was a pair like you two. Axel-Mindre, was his name. No wait, I took his name as my own, I mean. Axel-Sven. He was the first born, and when he died in battle on his raid near one Sir Daniel's lands. That's when I became Axel-Sven.

<u>Frey:</u>
No one noticed?

Frey felt rather stupid shortly after making his comment.
He knew the answer.

Axel-Sven:

He was my brother. The only difference between us was his
confidence. Unlike you two, where it's a little easier to tell.

Freya:
You would lie to the jarl?

Freya smiled in delight. She knew her father to be gullible,
but most would not attempt such as risky move on a jarl.

Frey:

He was the second born Freya. He didn't have much of an
inheritance. I would hope you would do the same if I were
to die.

Freya gave Frey a confused look.

Frey:
Scratch that. I mean if it were possible.

Jarl Lars had been listening in on the conversation, as he
had been hiding behind some trees in hopes of relieving
himself. He was surprised to hear this new information.
The jarl began to talk to himself.

Jarl Lars:

Those two. Is their loyalty in question? It's never been
before. And Axel-Sven. He's been lying for how many
years? Forget it. My business is with Sir Daniel. I'll sort
this out after.

Jarl Lars would come to regret those words.

XIX

ANANYA

A sudden rainstorm came upon the battlefield. The seer took the opportunity to delay the execution of the mercenary and Sir Daniel's inevitable demise.

Thyra:

This is a sign from the gods. We should retreat to camp and wait for the storm to settle.

Jarl Lars:

I'm done waiting seer! Sir Daniel's head will be mine!

Saint Gideon looked up toward the heavens and hoped it to be divine intervention.

St. Gideon:

I promise you, as God as my witness, if you take another step, it will be your last, jarl.

Surprised by his defeated foe, the jarl paid him no mind. He mockingly made a challenge to the God he didn't believe in.

Jarl Lars:
If your God is real, may he strike me down!

A Thunderclap silenced all at that moment. The sky turned a glaring white, blinding everyone. The smell of electricity permeated the air. The darkened sky appeared to shake the earth. Trembling, the Vikings hit the ground cowering over the uncontrollable and intangible power of the storm. Only Saint Gideon continued to observe the battlefield. His jaw stayed open with surprise to see the charred corpse of the jarl. Helga quickly ran to Leviticus to free him, afraid that a stray bolt may initiate his execution. Leviticus had hardly noticed her aid; he was too transfixed on the jarl. Sir Daniel shook off his amazement and signaled to his son to ready his bow once more. Saint Gideon stood with confidence and turned to face his enemies. He took a few steps toward them near the charred body of the jarl. He made a proclamation that shook the Vikings to their core.

St. Gideon:
WHO'S NEXT? WHO ELSE WILL CHALLENGE THE ONE TRUE GOD? HELL AWAITS YOU ALL! COME STEP FOREWARD.

The Vikings began to flee all at once. They were convinced that death was certain on this battlefield. Saint Gideon and his friends followed close behind in secret, hoping the enemy would not regroup. They stopped after hearing screams bellowing from the forest. The Norwegian reinforcements made their way to the manor as the sky began to clear up. Their leader sent her greetings.

<u>Jarl Brynhild:</u>
Our apologies for being late! We come bearing gold, and
the spoils of your enemies.

<u>Leviticus & Helga:</u>
It's about time!

Jarl Brynhild looked upon the charred remains of Jarl Lars.

<u>Jarl Brynhild:</u>
If it wasn't for this man, my people wouldn't have become
raiders. My husband wanted to put food on the table, so he
made his choice. I choose different.

<u>Dan:</u>
Well if Jarl Vidar was still around, I think we'd be having a
different conversation.

Sir Daniel elbowed his son in the ribs to silence him. He
did not want to insult his guests, especially not after being
rescued by them.

<u>Jarl Brynhild:</u>
I'm afraid you're right, young lad.

<u>Sir Daniel:</u>
So what's the occasion? A celebration?

<u>Jarl Brynhild:</u>
A wedding.

The jarl looked towards Leviticus's and Helga's direction. Both gave a look of surprise and excitement. Saint Gideon gave his thoughts to the situation, he worried for the dead.

St. Gideon:

We lost fifteen good men, Roberts included. I would like to hold a funeral when the time is right.

Jarl Brynhild was taken off guard by the announcement and gave her respect to Saint Gideon.

Jarl Brynhild:

Of course. I'll have my men bury them where you wish.

She gave Saint Gideon a concerned look. She noticed his scalped and gruesome head.

Jarl Brynhild:

Thyra, healers! Look at this man! Treat him well! We must act fast and tend to his injuries.

Saint Gideon was completely overwhelmed by the many women that came to his aid. They quickly knocked him down in their worry. They had thankfully caught him before more damage could be dealt. Thyra admired Saint Gideon for his bravery and faith. She marveled at his ability to call his God to action. She thought the divine needed motivation and bribes to be called upon. This was alien to her.

Thyra:

Your God is strong. I would like to know more about him when you're feeling better.

<u>St. Gideon:</u>
I'd be happy to tell you more about him…After my head
stops killing me.

Saint Gideon was overwhelmed by the events of the day, as
was all at the estate. He closed his eyes and tried to sleep
only to be awakened by Thyra.

<u>Thyra:</u>
YOUR HEAD IS INJURED! STAY AWAKE! YOUNG
FOOL!

XX

OAKEN

The body of Axel-Sven was not eaten by a bear but had floated down stream near shore. A lone Dane examines the body for any valuables. He knew a dead man had no need of possessions.

Gorva:

Not much, by the look of ya.

Gorva lifts the Viking up out of the stream. He was surprised to see the stranger spit up water.

Gorva:

You Dane?

Axel-Sven wondered what a Dane was, but he assumed it was important somehow. He wasn't sure who he was in the first place.

Axel-Sven:

Aye, Dane, be I. Sure why nooot.

Gorva:

You talk funny.

<u>Axel-Sven:</u>
But talk, yes.

<u>Gorva:</u>
What's your name.

Axel-Sven was silent for a while. Gorva soon realized that the man before him was more of a blank slate.

<u>Gorva:</u>
Fine will see about that later.

Axel-Sven shook his head in confirmation. Gorva sized up the Viking and made an offer.

<u>Gorva:</u>
Jarl Erik needs more men. Warriors. I can promise you a part of the spoils of the raiding party. We leave tomorrow if you want to run the paces.

Axel-Sven thought for a moment. He knew nothing of his former life. He had no aspirations or limitations. What was there to lose he, wagered.

<u>Axel-Sven:</u>
DEAL!

<u>Gorva:</u>
You seem slow to speak. Slow like an oak tree.

Axel-Sven looked at Gorva with a sense of satisfaction. He liked the sound of the word that had been spoken. He had found his name in a world he was just beginning to know.

Oaken.

XXI

PSALMS

Saint Gideon took a moment to gaze upon the monastery that stood before him. It was isolated from the mainland of Wessex and was a bastion against outside forces. Its modified basilica style architecture was something to behold.

Sir Dan:
This is where you'll be staying.

St. Gideon:
I'll try it, but I'm skeptical.

Sir Dan:
Well if you want to learn more Latin, read more scriptures, and have a good position –

St. Gideon:
Then I should work at Sir Daniels' Monastery.

Sir Dan:
Sir Dan's Monastery.

Saint Gideon gave a sigh and cleared his thoughts. It was hard to believe that Sir Daniel had died only three years prior.

Elder Quin:
He the new one?

The two were too busy conversing to notice the head monk meet them at the front entrance.

Sir Dan:
Yes, your replacement.

Elder Quin:
REPLACEMENT?!? ARE SAYING I'M OLD!

Elder Quin appeared as though his head was about to explode. Sir Dan tried to de-escalate the situation.

Sir Dan:
What? I was under the impression, that you would like to retire one day.

Elder Quin:
I'll retire when I'm dead! Who are you again?!?

Saint Gideon lifted an eyebrow, crossed his arms, and gave a very stern and commanding look to the elder.

St. Gideon:
He is the son of Sir Daniel. Show him respect.

Elder Quin was about to bow to show humility until he realized that he only did that to pray. He clapped his hands together and begged for mercy from his employer.

<u>Elder Quin:</u>
Please, forgive me. You haven't been here in so long I –

<u>Sir Dan:</u>
No, no. You're right. I was ten years old when I last visited. Letters don't exactly count either.

<u>Elder Quin:</u>
Let me rephrase. Please don't fire me. I want to work. There's always work to be done.

<u>Sir Dan:</u>
I acknowledge your skill; your management has been lacking as of late. The churches haven't been getting enough translations and our wealthy patrons have similar complaints.

Saint Gideon gave the elder a quick glance and saw a man about to lose everything that he devoted half his life to.

<u>St. Gideon:</u>
I accept this man's position. He will work under me. We will satisfy your requests, sir knight!

<u>Sir Dan:</u>
That's all I needed to hear. Well done brother.

<u>Elder Quin:</u>
Brother?

<u>Sir Dan:</u>
You don't see the resemblance?

Elder Quin made a confused face and motioned to the duo to make their way inside. They made their way into the atrium. A writing desk had been placed near the center with a feather, inkwell, and paper sitting on top.

<u>Elder Quin:</u>
Forgive me, there is a test. Sir Daniel started this practice. Translate the scripture before you if you wish to work.

Saint Gideon accepted the challenge. He began reading.

Venite, exultemus Domino;
iubilmus ad petram salutis
nostrae. Praeoccupemus eum
cum gratiarum atione et eum
in musica et cantu extollamus

Saint Gideon checked, then checked again. He was satisfied. He wrote his translation below the scripture.

Come, let us sing for joy
To the LORD; let us shout
Aloud to the Rock of our
Salvation. Let us come before him
with thanksgiving and extol
him with music and song

The new monk showed his work to the elder with anticipation. Elder Quin had begun to frown. He looked away and accepted his defeat.

91

<u>Elder Quin:</u>
You're hired.

XXII

LEVITICUS II

To Sir Dan,

I regret to hear about your father's untimely death. May you find it in your heart to forgive me.

<u>Levite:</u>
Father, play wi-me.

<u>Leviticus:</u>
Not right now son. Go find your mother.

The child ran off to search for his mother around the small humble cottage he knew as his home. Leviticus picked up where he left off.

The misses and I are retired as promised to us by your father.

But if you need anything do not hesitate to call on us.

Helga had snuck up of Leviticus and leaned on his rocking chair to get his attention.

Helga:

Where has that boy run off to?

Leviticus:

He was looking for you *good* Helga.

Helga smiled, crossing her arms, and wiggling her index finger to give her best know-it-all impression.

Helga:

I swear, that boy is attached to my hip.

Helga took a good look at the letter Leviticus was writing. She made her disapproval known and walked off to find her son.

The misses and I are retired as promised to us by your father.

But if you need anything do not hesitate to call on us.

Leviticus stopped for a moment to admire his wife and child gathering firewood in the distance. Such a strange and useful child he thought. Leviticus hated gathering firewood as a child.

Our child, Levite is growing to be a strong young lad.

I hope he becomes like you one day.

Without all the crying and whining.

I jest of course.

94

The warrior thought of his wife. He didn't like the idea of never going into battle again, but he also didn't want to leave his family without a head of the household. He made up his mind.

If you're ever in any danger, please hesitate to contact us for any help.

We a truly one hundred percent retired.

Give Saint Gideon my regards.

Hopefully you can beat him one day…God willing that is.

May God keep you,
Leviticus

Helga later that night double checked the letter. She acknowledged that Leviticus was the head of the household, but as husband and wife they were subject to one another. She often compared it to the relationship of the sword and shield.

<u>Helga:</u>
Let's see what the damage is. He better not have promised to go out of his way again. That man would have worked himself to death by now if not for me.

To some, Helga would be considered nosy. To Leviticus, she was like his anchor at sea. She completed him.

To Sir Dan,

I regret to hear about your father's untimely death. May you find it in your heart to forgive me.

The misses and I are retired as promised to us by your father.

~~But if you need anything do not hesitate to call on us.~~

Our child, Levite is growing to be a strong young lad.

I hope he becomes like you one day.

Without all the crying and whining.

I jest of course.

If you're ever in any danger, please hesitate to contact us for any help.

We a truly one hundred percent retired.

Give Saint Gideon my regards.

Hopefully you can beat him one day...God willing that is.

May God keep you,
Leviticus

<u>Helga:</u>
Perfect! That was the last of our paper anyway.

97

The
Author

JOSHUA JOSEPH
MONTEJANO
J.J.M.

First, I want to thank you for taking the time to read my book.

I was inspired by the art of the Medieval Ages and the historical significance of the Viking Age. A time full of adversity and new challenges. I practice sword & buckler in my free time, so I wanted to incorporate this element.

I also was inspired by certain decorative elements of the Middle Ages like reliquaries, basilica themed churches, and the many colorful manuscripts scribes and monks had to translate.

It was challenging to write a story in which people weren't simply bad or good. People are imperfect and there's a thin line between good and evil that is often overgeneralized when it comes to works of fiction. I wrote Helga to be help be the bridge between some of the Vikings. She's been on both sides.

Leviticus was more of neutral character. He fights for coin, but his loyalty has always been to Sir Daniel.

I wanted Roberts to be a more complex character. He is defined by his trauma, but still has a certain level of character growth.

Saint Gideon, I originally implemented to be a man that had lots of potential and treaded the waters lightly. As a Haitian man in a foreign land, I thought he could show a different perspective to the narrative.

Sir Daniel has a certain sense of justice to him, even if he will often get himself in harm's way for others.

Dan was introduced to add more of a younger inexperienced perspective to the whole of the story.

The twins, Freya, and Frey, I added in since I am a twin myself. I thought their dynamic could help add more to the overall story.

Thank you again and God bless.

ACKNOWLEDGEMENT

Thank you for being my editor, bro. I'd like to dedicate this book to my family for always supporting me, and to God for the air in my lungs as well as for any inspiration he's given me along the way.

P.S.

All biblical quotes come from more modern interpretations of the Bible like the NIV version. This is done for clarity and not for the authenticity of the manuscript translations. The sword and buckler techniques used are inspired by fighting treatises like I.33 Sword and Buckler Manuscript.

The following is a work of fiction inspired by the historical period known as the Viking Age.

Life was hard. People fought to survive the untamed, natural world.

Cultures clashed. Lives were lost. Cruelties were justified in the brutality of war.

The faith and reason of the people were tested beyond what they could have possibly imagined.

This was the time where everything was filled with uncertainty.

This book is a prequel and takes place eight years before *Blade, Buckler, Bastion/Blade, Buckler, Bastion: The Illuminated Edition.*

It is not essential to read this book first since the events contained are referenced in part, and without spoilers in the next book.

Regardless, this is the first in the book series entitled *Blade, Buckler, Bastion.*

A lone survivor of Viking conquest finds refuge under the care of the knight, Sir Daniel.

For eight long years, Saint Gideon is raised to combat the Viking threat to Wessex and Mercia.

With the help of his mentor, Leviticus, and aid from his new brother, Dan, will these warriors avenge their fellow countrymen?

Or will this endeavor lead to an early grave?